SYMPHONY CITY

Written and illustrated by **AMY MARTIN**

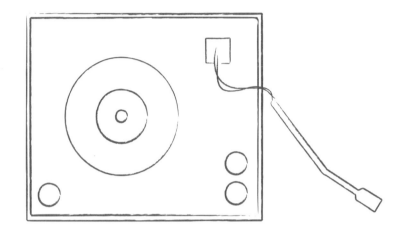

FOR

Robert Van Allsburg,
who gave me sheet music for every birthday
&
Esther Tanis Van Allsburg,
who taught me how to draw

nothing to do

the station is empty at first

then the train comes and it is very crowded

but I let go

there are too many people

and then no one

hello!

SYMPHONY STREET

I can find my own way.

if I follow the sound

up to the city

there is music around every corner

it comes from the street

and fills the sky

it pours in waves

through open windows

and expands

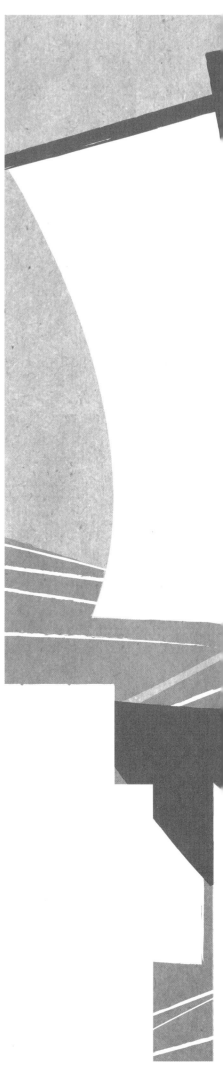

it starts as a sprout

and bursts into a forest

it drifts through the trees

and soars over the city

it leaps and spins

across the rooftops

even the moon wants to listen

and under the stars

and streetlamps

there is color everywhere

until the streets become quiet again

but not everyone is asleep

the

best

songs

love

you

back

AMY MARTIN
was raised in Michigan and studied at the University of Michigan School of Art & Design.
She spent the first part of her career designing magazines and newspapers, including
The Advocate, *The Detroit Free Press*, and *The Los Angeles Times*.
She has since created work for 826LA, *The San Francisco Panorama*,
Public Option Please, *The New York Times*, *Foreign Policy Magazine*, Knock Knock,
Death Cab for Cutie, and Band of Horses. Her posters have been shown
at Manifest Hope, Re:Form School, and the 2010 California Design Biennial.

She always cries at rock shows. This is her first book.

THANK YOU
Symphony City was made in kitchens, hotels and guest rooms in Los Angeles, Detroit,
Grand Rapids, Ann Arbor, Big Sur, San Francisco, Portland, Seattle, and Vancouver, and on trains in between.
It would not have existed without help and encouragement from Keith Barry, Michael Bolger, Lewisa Bradley,
John Bradley, Wayne DeSelle, Mary Ann Gallo, Michael Benjamin Lerner, Maren Levinson,
Kara Martin, Amiee McCrea, Morgan Phillips, Rachael Porter, Amy Raasch, Emiliana Sandoval,
Robbie Thompson, Chris Walla & DCfC, Zeitgeist Artist Management,
The Silverlake Conservatory of Music, and 826LA.

There are nineteen cats in this book.
Their names are Catsnacks, Gigi #1, Gigi #2, Hazel, Hairball, Hoo-Hah, Jitters,
Killer, Little Green, Pauline, Pickle, Princess Angel Fur, Senator Fancy Claws,
Snowpants, Sparky, Starbuck, Sweet Lou, Tiny Man, and Weasel.

**McSWEENEY'S
McMULLENS**

www.mcsweeneys.net

ISBN: 978-1-936365-39-5
First edition